Oni and the
Kingdom of Onion

By Marc Rubenstein

Oni and the Kingdom of Onion

By Marc Rubenstein

NEW YORK

LONDON • NASHVILLE • MELBOURNE • VANCOUVER

Oni and the Kingdom of Onion

Published in New York, New York, by Morgan James Publishing. Morgan James is a trademark of Morgan James, LLC. www.MorganJamesPublishing.com

The Morgan James Speakers Group can bring authors to your live event. For more information or to book an event visit The Morgan James Speakers Group at www.TheMorganJamesSpeakersGroup.com.

ISBN 9781642790573 paperback
ISBN 9781642790580 case laminate
ISBN 9781642790597 eBook
Library of Congress Control Number: 2018905919

Cover and Interior Design by:
Tamra Gerard

Illustrations by:
Hannah Miller & Noelle Richardson

In an effort to support local communities, raise awareness and funds, Morgan James Publishing donates a percentage of all book sales for the life of each book to Habitat for Humanity Peninsula and Greater Williamsburg.

Get involved today! Visit
www.MorganJamesBuilds.com

A message to the readers of *Oni and the Kingdom of Onion:*

Hi, my name is Tom Thorkelson. My passion in life is bringing to the faith community respect for those who differ in their beliefs. If the people of the world followed the true tenants of their faith, and the lessons shared in this book, this would be a better world for all. Rabbi Marc Rubenstein has chosen to use the ingredients of salads as a way to help children understand the value of cooperation.

This children's story highlights that while people (salad ingredients) are indeed different shapes, colors, sizes - even textures - we can work peacefully together and enrich each other (as the characters do), and that rather than being in conflict, we can make this world one of peace, compassion, safety.

We can, like the ingredients of a salad, retain our individuality, character, and taste, while working together to create a better and more spiritually nourished world.

TOM THORKELSON

Vice-President, Orange County Interfaith Network and Interfaith Activist

ABOUT THE AUTHOR:

Rabbi Marc Rubenstein is an active and enthusiastic educator with a Master's of Arts Degree from New York University. He has taught a world's religions class at the University of California, Berkeley. He is a member of the Teacher's Association and National Association of Temple Educators. Currently, Rabbi Marc is a professor at the House of Judaism teaching morals and ethics to students from all over the world, many of whom have different faiths and religious beliefs. His passion is to share wisdom of how to help make the world a safer and more peaceful place for all!

ABOUT THE EXECUTIVE EDITOR

Evan James Sillings is a professional writer and story development editor from Newport Beach, California. This is his second collaboration with his longtime friend and colleague Marc Rubenstein. Their first book together, *Weddings By the Glass*, like this one, is meant to inspire, entertain, and inform. Evan is a lover of stories, told in any form, just as long as they are well told. The melody and harmony of words put together artfully brings him great joy. He hopes this book brings enjoyment to all!

ABOUT THE ARTIST

Tamra Gerard was raised in Southern California and was introduced to the arts by her mother who would often take her to museums, street fairs and galleries exposing her to a broad spectrum of art. At age six, Tamra's painting "Dog with Pink Eyes" was accepted into the Laguna Arts Festival in Laguna Beach, California. In 1985 she received an art degree from Cal State University, Fullerton. Today Tamra is a commissioned oil painter specializing in animal portraits, award-winning graphic designer and muralist with a passion for the oil medium. Painting has become a large part of her everyday life and she infuses it into graphic design as much as possible. Tamra can be reached at TamraGerardArt.com and followed on lnstagram-TamraGerard.

ABOUT THE ILLUSTRATOR

Hannah Miller is in the 8th grade at Orange County School of the Arts in Santa Ana, California. She was recently accepted into their Digital Media Conservatory beginning next fall, her freshman year. "Oni and the Kingdom of Onion" is her first work as a children's book illustrator. Hannah loves vegetables, and she is thrilled for this opportunity! Her dream after high school is to study animation at CalArts in Valencia, California.

ABOUT THE LAYOUT PRODUCER

Beverly Nixon is a mother of a blended family in Utah who recently converted to Judaism with the guidance of Rabbi Marc. Even though she is an ex-Catholic and her husband and step-kids are Mormon, she has found love and support in her new Jewish community and happily volunteers at her local synagogue. She is proud of her Mexican heritage and has a passion for oil painting.

Why I Wrote
Oni and the Kingdom of Onion

I have taught children most of my life, including three of my own. When I go into homes, I see the same words written on most refrigerators: Respect others, share, tell the truth, and be kind. The world today is a dangerous place to live. Anger and hate are abundant. As a rabbi and teacher, I have the ability to teach people how to think about today's problems.

In a salad, every ingredient in the salad needs the other ingredients to make it tasty. Each vegetable or fruit in the salad has virtually no enjoyable taste by itself when eaten. It takes all of the ingredients to make it work. Consider as well this point: There is peace and harmony in a salad and no name-calling. People can learn from this. In the course of human history, even in the world today, there is always imminent danger of conflict. There is not a generation in the history of mankind that has not experienced tragedy, violence, and war.

This is the reason why Oni was created. In addition, consider the following points:

1. The word Oni (prounced Ahni in Hebrew) means the pronoun "I" or simply "me," that is, every individual.
2. The book ends with the saying, there is even peace in me. We all have the ability to make the world a better place to live if we follow the 4 rules on the refrigerator. These rules are the basis of most of all the world's religions!
3. The onion has layers to it with no core at its center. We can change are views. No one should hate a person on the basis of or because of his race, religion or beliefs.
4. There really was a Kingdom of Onion where Jews in Egypt lived in peace.
5. I hope you enjoy reading this fun children's book over and over again, gain wisdom from its content, and share it with your family and friends!

All the Best,
Rabbi Marc.

BE
KIND

ALWAYS
SHARE

TELL THE
TRUTH

RESPECT
EVERYONE AND THEIR DIFFERENCES

Tears filled Carli Carrot's eyes

as she put her iPad down.

"What's wrong?" asked Oni Onion.

"There's fighting everywhere," cried Carli.

"People are mean to each other and hurt each other.

It's sad."

1

Oni put his arm around Carli.

"I know. It's terrible.

You'd think everyone could get along, like us.

Even the children in our home

fight with each other."

"What's going on?"

interrupted Tommy Tomato.

"I was explaining how vegetables

all get along," said Oni.

"It's a shame that people can't do the same."

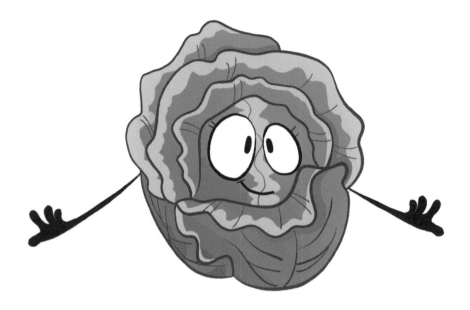

Lucy Lettuce rolled over to her friends,

"That's right. I saw the same thing on my iPad.

It's outrageous.

We're all shapes and sizes.

We're different colors, but we don't fight.

We help each other."

Oni shook his head.

"No one has ever told me I stink. And,

no one tells Bell Pepper she's too plump.

We're kind to each other. We share. We tell the truth.

And, we respect each other."

"That's right," said Garret Garlic

as he put his hands on his hips.

"In our salad, we work together. We don't try to be better

or stronger than the other vegetables."

"Yes!" said Oni.

"We enhance each other's flavor.

We create a super-cool salad."

Lucy waved her hands in the air.

"Yeah! Every ingredient in a salad is special.

We have our own flavor, texture,

smell, and look."

Oni nodded. "That's right.

And, sometimes nuts, fruits, breads, and my silly friend

Peter Pineapple come to visit.

We don't tell them to get out. We don't fight with them.

We know it makes our salad more fun."

"I think it has to do with being humble

and respectful," said Carli.

"Oni, you have a sacred history. You could feel that you're

better than someone else. But, you don't."

Garret burrowed his brows.

"What do you mean,

Oni could feel haughty?"

"Well," said Oni as he answered for Carli.

"My history goes back to THE FIRST HANNUKAH.

In fact, I was named after Onias.

He built a Temple in Alexandria, Egypt."

"I didn't know that," said Lucy.

"Me, either," said Tommy.

"Tell us how . . . pleeeassse."

"Sure," said Oni. They all got comfortable.

"You see, it started a LONG time ago.

There were two Jewish brothers, Onias and Tobias.

They had a huge fight."

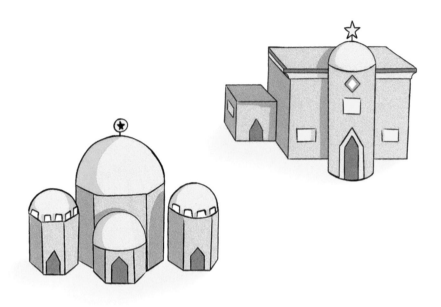

"The fight was so bad," said Oni,

"that the brothers took their families and

moved to different lands.

And, they built two different temples."

"Whoa," said Tommy.

"Yeah," said Oni. "Tobias build a Temple in Jerusalem

and Onias built a Temple in

the Kingdom of Onion."

Getting interested in the story, Garret raised his hand.

"Why'd they fight?"

Oni shrugged. "Don't know."

Oni went on.

"Anyway, even though the brothers didn't see each other,

they wrote letters."

"But," said Oni,

"while Onias was at peace in Egypt,

Tobias and his followers had a hard time in Israel.

It was because of a Greek named Antiochus."

Carli shook her head. "That's terrible. What happened?"

"Well," said Oni, "Antiochus was mean, especially to Jews.

He closed their temple.

He didn't care about God's truth or Torah."

Tommy's eyes grew wide. "That's awful.

The Jews must have been sad."

"They were," said Oni. "Both in Israel and Egypt."

A slow smile crept up on Oni's face.

"But, Judah Maccabee came to the rescue.

He was a follower of Tobias and lead a revolt against Antiochus.

After battling for three years, the Jews in Israel finally

drove Antiochus away."

"Yea!" yelled Lucy!

"Yeah," echoed the others.

Oni got up and stretched.

"Israel was at peace again."

"They were so happy," said Oni,

"they sent a letter to Onias and the Jews in Alexandria.

They asked if the Kingdom of Onion would come celebrate

the rededication of their Temple."

Carli put her hands on her cheeks.

"Did they accept the invitation?"

"They sure did," said Oni.

"They wanted to celebrate Israel's victory over Antiochus."

"Good," said Garret.

Lucy smacked her lips. "Hmph.

It was about time they got back together!"

"Now to finish up," said Oni. "It was the year before ZERO.

The two kingdoms got together and had an

ENORMOUS FEAST.

It became the first HANNUKAH!"

"Onias brought a gift of oil

to light the menorah for this very special occasion,"

said Oni. "It was from the original Temple

in Jerusalem."

"Yea!" yelled the vegetables. "Everyone was happy!"

"And, everyone got along," said Oni.

"Just like the ingredients of a BIG salad."

שָׁלוֹם

Oni sat back down. "Whew! That was a long story.

Hey, did you know that the secret recipe for peace is to say,

'SHALOM'? Peace is inside ALL of us.

Peace is even in me, an onion."

HISTORICAL TIMELINE OF EVENTS

From the time of the giving of the Torah on Mount Sinai to the first Hannukah,
the historical events happened in this way:

1. The Priesthood of Israel is traced from the time of Aaron, Moses's brother over 2250 years ago, to the time of King David, who appointed the high priest Zadok.
2. Alexander the Great conquers Jerusalem in the year 331 BCE.
3. About 150 years later the Priesthood divides over a fight between the high priest Tobias and the rival contender, his brother, the high priest Onias (175 BCE). The conflict is not resolved.
4. Onias and his many followers move to Egypt and found the Kingdom of Onion (The historian Josephus states in his book entitled *The History of the Jews*).
5. In 168 BCE the Greek king Antiochus invades Israel and changes the reigning priest Menelaus to his own high priest, Jason, who abandons Jewish laws and customs. After that the Temple in Jerusalem is desecrated.
6. The Maccabees rebel and lead a revolt. There is fighting all over Israel for 3 years. The Temple in Jerusalem is restored by Antiochus and then is rededicated in 165 BCE. Rededication in Hebrew means Hannukah when translated into Hebrew! Thus the derivation of the holiday.
7. In the year 165 BCE the fighting finally ends! Peace and happiness are everywhere. Lots of love, happiness, sharing, and joy!
8. The Hannukah celebration is decreed.
9. Onias the high priest and tens of thousands of Jews from Egypt are invited to celebrate the first Hannukah.
10. Onias brings oil from the Kingdom of Onion to celebrate the first Hannukah in Jerusalem and the first lighting of the Hannukah menorah. The Entire Jewish community of Egypt and Israel attend (Rabbi Stephen M. Wylen's book entitled *The Jews in the Time of Jesus*).

CPSIA information can be obtained
at www.ICGtesting.com
Printed in the USA
BVHW021213251118
533908BV00018B/392/P

9 781642 790573